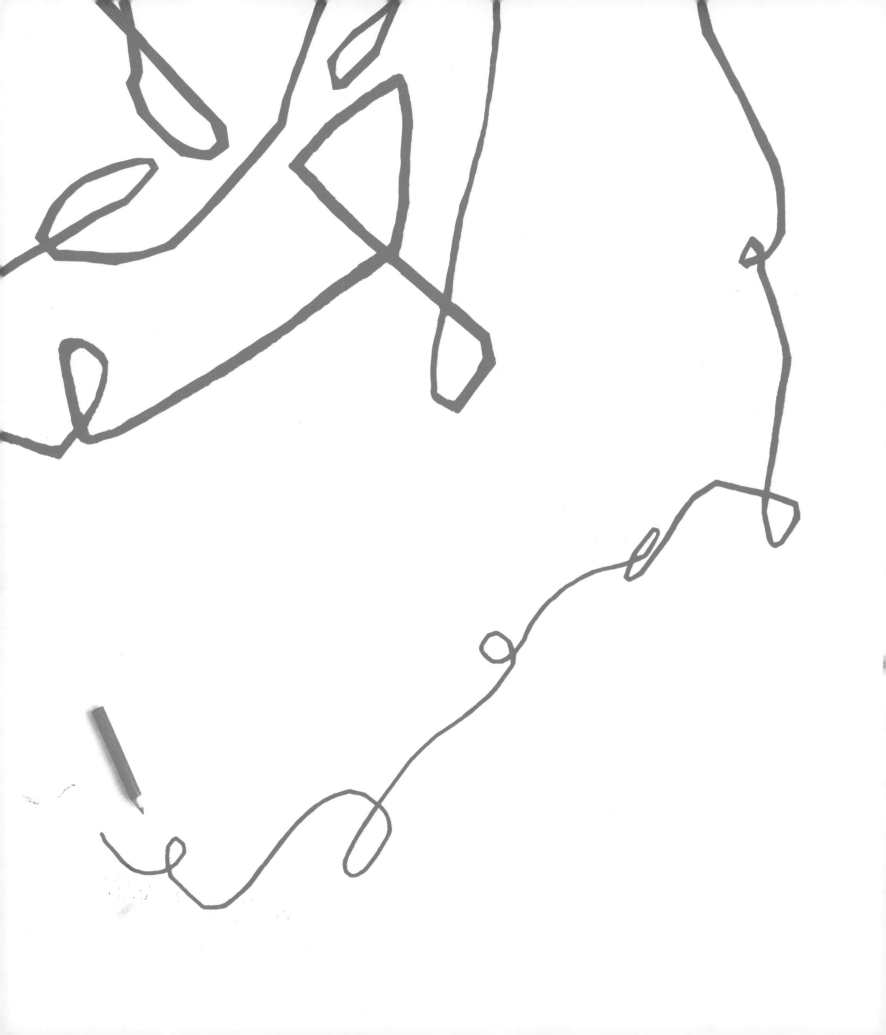

Lauren Child

A Dog with NICE ears

Featuring *Charlie and Lola*

CANDLEWICK PRESS

For
Josey

18 19 20 21 22 23 APS 10 9 8 7 6 5 4 3 2 1

Printed in Humen, Dongguan, China

This book was typeset in ITC Officina Serif.

The illustrations were done in mixed media.

The dog drawings on the endpapers
were actually done by Tuesday.

Candlewick Press
99 Dover Street
Somerville, Massachusetts 02144

visit us at www.candlewick.com

Library of Congress Catalog Card Number pending
ISBN 978-1-5362-0036-2

First published in Great Britain in 2017
by The Watts Publishing Group

First U.S. edition 2018

I have this little sister, Lola.
She is small and very funny.
At the moment, all Lola can talk about is dogs.
She says she would like one more than anything you
could ever think of.

"More than a squirrel or an **actual** fox," she says.

Mostly we both talk about what **sort** of
dog she would choose if Mom and Dad
didn't always say . . .

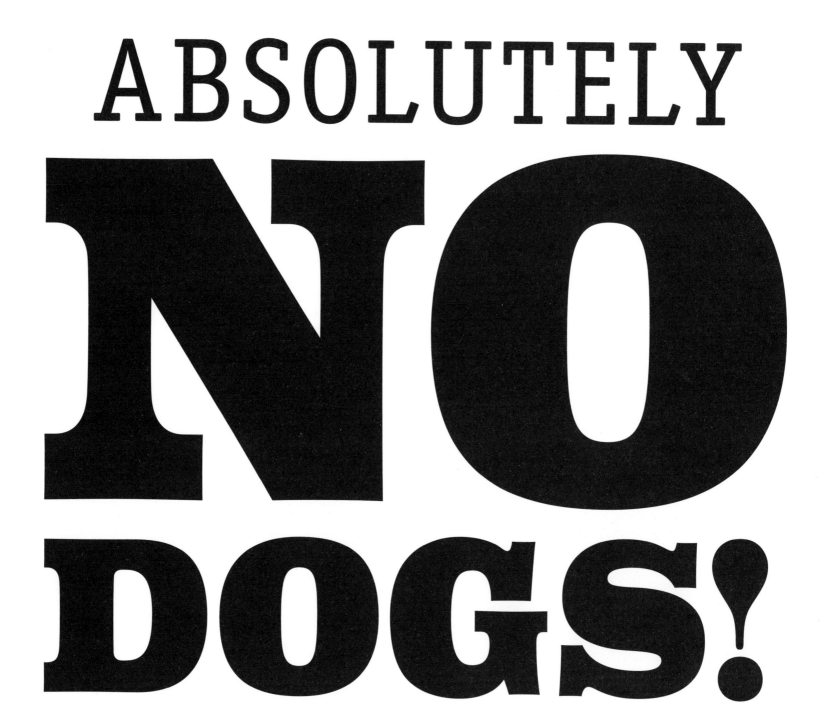

Lola says,

"It's **NOT fair.**
Charlie's friend
Marv has
a **dog.**"

Dad says,
"Lucky Marv."

Mom says,
"How about a rabbit, Lola?"
I say, "A rabbit is NOT the **same** as a dog."

Lola says,

"It is **not EVEN**
the **same as**
a squirrel."

Dad says he can take Lola to the pet shop one Saturday, and she can choose WHICHEVER rabbit she wants. Lola says, "OK."

I say,
"But, Lola,
you do NOT want
a rabbit."

And
Lola says,
"Don't
worry,
I WILL
choose
a dog."

I would get
A BROWN DOG
because my friend
Marv has a brown
dog and they are
the **best** kind
of dog.

Lola thinks so too.
She wants to call it Snowpuff.

But I say,
"That is NOT a **good** name
for a BROWN dog."

Lola says,
"But SNOW is **nice**
and I LIKE
the **word**
'**PUFF!**'"

This is NOT a good reason
to call a **brown** dog
Snowpuff.

Lola says,
"It MUST have nice ears
because EARS are important.
You hold your
glasses on with
your ears."

I say,
"But, Lola, a dog
wouldn't NEED glasses."

"How do
you
know?"
she says.

I say,
"Have you ever **seen**
a dog wearing GLASSES?"

She says,
"No, BUT they

probably only

wear them

FOR

reading."

"What about its TAIL?" I say.
"Tails are **important** for dogs.
They use their tails to tell you
how they are FEELING."

Lola says,
"If I had
a **tail**,
I would have
a
b^ushyish
tail like a FOX.

But my friend Lotta would most probably have a featherish tail like a BIRD."

I say, "Lola, we are talking about a tail for a DOG."

Lola says,
"Well then,
a **waggy one**
of course."

I say,
"That is the **only**
sensible thing you
have said so far."

Lola says, "YES,
it must be VERY
waggy

and FIVE **rulers** long."

I say, "NO dog has a tail

as

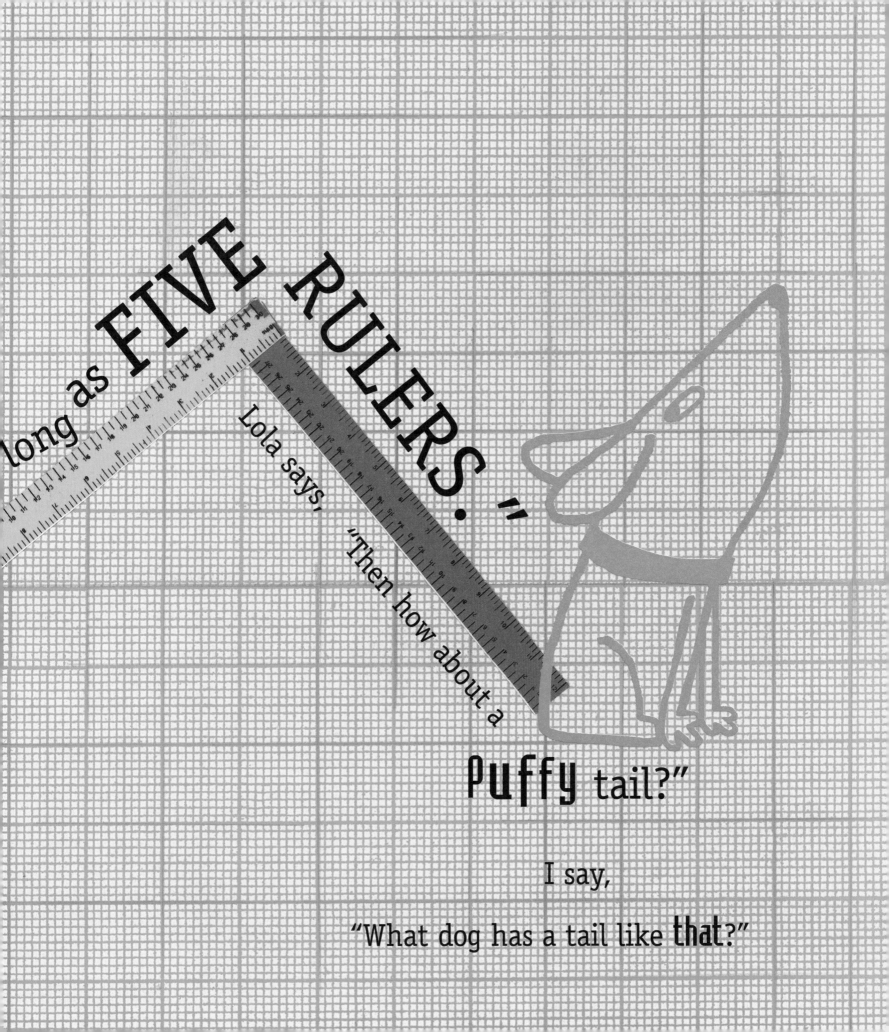

long as **FIVE RULERS."**

Lola says,

"Then how about a

Puffy tail?"

I say,

"What dog has a tail like **that**?"

Lotta says,
"An extremely **furryish** dog has a puffy tail."

Lola says,
"Oh yes, it MUST have
**extremely furry
fur.**"

"Furrier than a **poodle**?"
says Lotta.

"Yes,
not like
a POODLE,"
says Lola.

"More like
a Pekingese?"
I say.

"Like a cat,"
says Lola.

I say, "I hope you
don't want a dog
that meows."

bar**k**

Lola says,
"Of course our dog must NOT be a meower. It must absolutely do barking."

"Good!" I say. "Barking is BEST for a dog."

SNIFF,

SNIFF,

SNIFF

"YES," says Lola, "and it must be very,
VERY QUIET BARKING
so it does not wake us up."
"But barking is meant to wake us up," I say.
Lola says,
"Our dog can wake us up with sniffing."

Marv says,
"Dogs do like to sniff."

Cha_e

"So it should have a
wiggly nose,"
says Lola.

I say,
"Do dogs have **wiggly** noses?"

"Only if they have an ITCH,"
says Marv.

"Oh, I don't **want** an ITCHY dog," I say.

Marv says,
"They only itch if
they catch fleas."

"**MY DOG
MUST NOT
catch
fleas,**"

says Lola.

"He must catch **sticks.**"

Marv says,
"It can be ANY color you want and have ANY ears you like. But whatever dog you get, it MUST be a dog with short legs. Dogs with short legs do less walking."

Lola says, "Why don't we get a **dog** with **three legs,**

like Mrs. Hansen's one? He **only hops.**

"It might be **tricky** to find a dog with LESS than four legs," I say.

"But a **hopping dog** would be **nice**," says Lola.

"You are going to have the weirdest dog," says Marv.

On Saturday
Lola gets up early.
"Where are
you going?"
I say.

"I am **going** to the **pet shop**," she says.

"To get a rabbit?" I ask.

"**NO**,"

she says,

"**I TOLD you.**

I am going to

fetch

My dog."

When Lola comes home she is carrying a big box.
"I can't hear any barking," I say.

"No, THIS **dog** is
more of **a sniffer**,"
says Lola.

"It sounds like
it's HOPPING," I say.

"EXACTLY,"
says Lola.
"I **won't** even HAVE to
train it."

I peek inside.
"That's not a **brown** dog,"
I say.

"NO, it is **slightly more** GRAY," says Lola.
"They did not have any **brown** ones with
nice ears."

I say,
"Lola, THAT dog looks
like a **rabbit.**"

"**I know!**"
says Lola.

"It's
BECAUSE of
the **wiggly**
nose."

"And maybe
the **puffy** tail,"
I say.

"What should we call him?" she says.

I say, "How about SNOWPUFF?"

"Yes,
Snowpuff
is a
go**o**d na**m**e
for **a**
DOG
with  nice
e**a**r**s**."

31901063012902